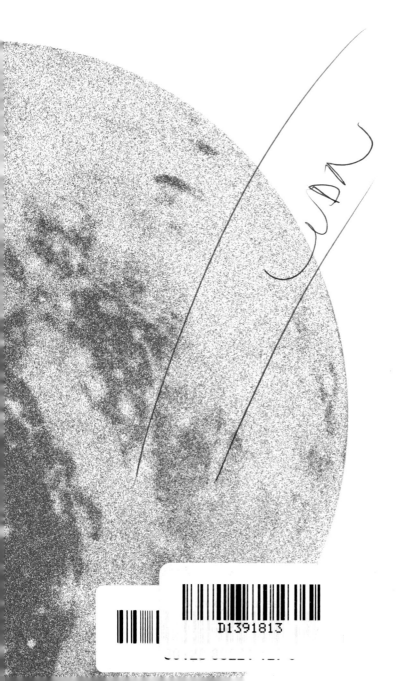

Space Quest:

Jump to Jupiter

By Peter Lock

Series Editor Deborah Lock
Editor Arpita Nath
Project Art Editor Hoa Luc
Art Editor Rashika Kachroo
DTP Designers Ashok Kumar and Anita Yadav
Picture Researcher Surya Sankash Sarangi
Producer, Pre-production Ben Marcus
Managing Editor Soma B. Chowdhury
Managing Art Editor Ahlawat Gunjan
Art Director Martin Wilson

Reading Consultant
Shirley Bickler

First published in Great Britain by
Dorling Kindersley Limited
80 Strand, London, WC2R 0RL

A CIP catalogue record for this book
is available from the British Library

ISBN: 978-0-2411-8284-0

Printed and bound in China.

The publisher would like to thank the following for their kind permission
to reproduce their photographs:
(Key: a-above; b-below/bottom; c-centre; f-far; l-left; r-right; t-top)
1 NASA: ESA and E. Karkoschka (U. Arizona) (t). 4-5 NASA: JPL-Caltech / SETI Institute. 5 Science Photo Library: Roger Harris (c).
6 NASA: JPL-Caltech. 6-61 Dreamstime.com: Clearviewstock (b). 7 Dreamstime.com: Julien Tromeur (br). 8-9 Alamy Images: Paul Fleet (t).
9 Dreamstime.com: Julien Tromeur (br). 10-11 Corbis: Denis Scott. 12-13 Alamy Images: Gl0ck. 14 Getty Images: Juan Gartner.
14-15 NASA: JPL-Caltech / SETI Institute. 15 Alamy Images: Gl0ck (c). Getty Images: Juan Gartner (cla). NASA: HiRISE-J MRO / LPL (U.
Arizona) (cra). 16 NASA: JPL-Caltech (t). 17 Corbis: Denis Scott (b). 18 Dreamstime.com: Julien Tromeur (bl). 19 Corbis: NASA - digital
version copyright / Science Faction (t). 20 Dreamstime.com: Julien Tromeur (bl). 21 NASA: (t). 23 Dreamstime.com: Alexokokok (c/Frame).
NASA: (t). 24 Corbis: (crb). 24-25 NASA: JPL-Caltech / SETI Institute. 25 NASA: ESA and E. Karkoschka (U. Arizona). 26 Corbis: Ron
Miller / Stocktrek Images (t). 28-29 Corbis: Denis Scott (t). 28 Alamy Images: RGB Ventures / SuperStock (t). 29 NASA: ESA and E.
Karkoschka (U. Arizona) (tr). 30-31 NASA and The Hubble Heritage Team (AURA/STScI). 31 Dreamstime.com: Julien Tromeur (br).
34-35 NASA: (c); JPL-Caltech / SETI Institute. 36-37 NASA: JPL-Caltech / SETI Institute. 38 Alamy Images: Tristan3D (tl).
40 Corbis: NASA - JPL / Science Faction (ca). Dreamstime.com: Alexokokok (t/Frame). 41 Dreamstime.com: Julien Tromeur (br).
42-43 Corbis: NASA - JPL / Science Faction. 44-45 Alamy Images: Trevor Smithers ARPS. 45 Dreamstime.com: Julien Tromeur (br).
46-47 NASA: (Jupiter's moons); JPL-Caltech / SETI Institute. 46 Alamy Images: Science Photo Library (b). Corbis: NASA-JPL-Caltech -
digital versi / Science Faction (crb). 47 Alamy Images: NASA / World History Archive & ARPL (b). Corbis: (ca); NASA-JPL-Caltech -
digital versi / Science Faction (cla); NASA / Roger Ressmeyer (cb). NASA: JPL / University of Arizona / University of Colorado (bc).
48 Alamy Images: NASA / World History Archive & ARPL (tl). Corbis: Denis Scott (t/Background). 50 Alamy Images: NG Images.
52 Corbis: NASA / epa (c). 53 Dreamstime.com: Julien Tromeur (br). 54 Alamy Images: Martin Almqvist (t). 56-57 Alamy Images: Zoonar
GmbH (t). 58 123RF.com: Urs Flueeler (clb). Corbis: Logan Mock-Bunting (cla). Dreamstime.com: Eric Isselee (br)
Jacket images: Front: Dreamstime.com: Surachet Khamsuk / Surachetkhamsuk tr. Back: Dorling Kindersley: NASA tl.
Dreamstime.com: Clearviewstock (background). Spine: Dorling Kindersley: NASA / JPL.
All other images © Dorling Kindersley
For further information see: www.dkimages.com

A WORLD OF IDEAS:
SEE ALL THERE IS TO KNOW

www.dk.com

Contents

Year 2052 Space Quest Mission Update

Two years ago, five brave astronauts and a pet rabbit set out on Space Quest. Their mission was to visit the planets of the solar system. Their first stage to Mars is completed. Now they are on their way to Jupiter.

Mission team

Name	Age	Role
Ned Crater	43	Commander
Flo Comet	34	Engineer
Alex Nova	37	Lander pilot
Izzy Stardust	31	Science officer
Lem Cosmos	30	Engineer
Coconut	5	Pet rabbit

Mission aims

- to collect samples,
- to carry out experiments,
- to set up life-supporting bases if possible.

The spacecraft *Ramesses* was built section by section in Earth's outer atmosphere. The astronauts reached *Ramesses* in a rocket.

Technical data

Ramesses is designed to transport the astronauts through the solar system. Separate landers, such as *Juba*, interlock with *Ramesses*.

Rocky Ride

"Hold on tight! We're entering the asteroid belt," said Ned to his crewmates. He gripped the control lever firmly.

"We're in for a rocky ride," joked Lem.

The crew laughed as rocks of all shapes and sizes whizzed

past them. Ned guided the spacecraft *Ramesses* through the spaces between them.

"Look! That asteroid looks like a giant potato!" exclaimed Alex.

"You're always thinking of food," remarked Flo. "Asteroids are covered in craters and troughs where they crashed into each other."

The **asteroid belt** is a large ring of rocks that circles around the Sun between Mars and Jupiter.

"Crashed!" repeated Alex.

"Don't worry, Alex," said Izzy, stroking Coconut on her lap. "Asteroids orbit the Sun just like Earth and the other planets do. A collision only happens every now and then. The gravity of Jupiter is very strong and its pull sometimes knocks one out of orbit. The asteroid spins off into space. It may collide with other

asteroids or even a planet."

"They're more spaced out than I thought they'd be," said Ned, calmly. He guided *Ramesses* around the asteroids as if playing a computer game.

Scientists calculate there are about 1.4 million rocks in the **asteroid belt**.

"It's still like being pelted at by fast-moving tennis balls," remarked Alex, nervously.

"No wonder!" said Flo. "Some of those rocks are flashing past us at five kilometres per second. They go at different speeds though and some move in wobbly twists because of their strange shapes."

Ahead of them, a large, round, white shape appeared.

"That's Ceres!" pointed out Izzy. "It's an icy dwarf planet — a leftover from when the main planets were formed millions of years ago. It may have more fresh water on it than on Earth."

"Whoah!" cried Lem.

In the distance, an asteroid
suddenly changed direction
and hurtled into another. Rocks
went flying in every direction.
A huge piece headed straight
for *Ramesses*.

"I can't avoid it in time.
Any ideas anyone?" asked Ned.

"I'll blast it apart with the laser cannon," suggested Alex.

"Crazy! But it could be our only way through," replied Ned.

Alex switched on the laser cannon and aimed it at the centre of the rock. His heartbeat quickened as his sweaty hands held the firing lever.

Asteroids Close Up

Are these the pieces that tried to form planets billions of years ago?

Uneven surface

Crater

Look at the evidence:

- uneven shapes with craters where collisions have happened
- some are balls of rubble where fragments have clumped together
- they follow orbital paths around the Sun
- some even have small moons of their own orbiting them

Are all asteroids grey?

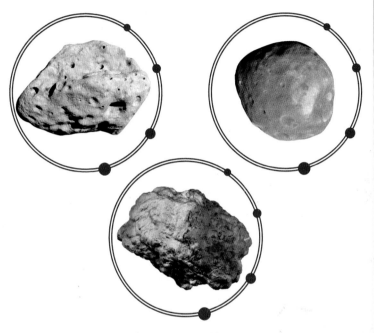

The most common asteroids are grey.
They are rocky, and are found on
the outer areas of the asteroid belt.
Other asteroids can be greenish
to reddish in colour. These contain
some metals, and are found on the
inner areas of the belt. The asteroids
made of metals are red, and are found
in the middle areas of the belt.

Stepping Out

FLASH!

Alex fired the laser. It zapped the huge rock, splitting it in two. The spacecraft jerked as Ned swerved *Ramesses* between the two parts. Clouds of rock dust covered the window, blocking the view.

Clunk! Clunk!

Small pieces of rock pounded the sides of the spacecraft. Ned tried to dodge as many as he could see. Izzy held Coconut tightly.

As the dust cloud cleared, the black of space surrounded them.

"We're through the asteroid belt," sighed Flo with relief.

"That was a hair-raising ride!" said Lem with relief. "I didn't need to comb my hair this morning."

"All that jumping around and being pelted by rocks may have caused some damage," remarked Ned.

"I'll go outside and check *Ramesses'* bodywork," offered Flo. She headed for the exit capsule to get ready for the EVA.

EVA means extravehicular activity. This refers to any activity by an astronaut outside the spacecraft such as a space walk.

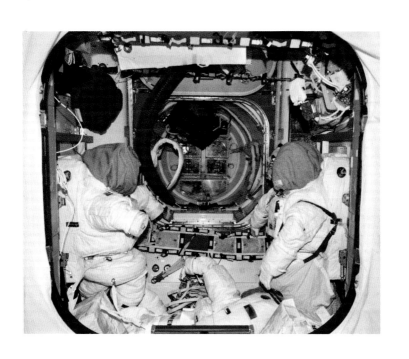

Izzy laid Coconut into the space hutch and went to help her. Alex also helped Flo into the EVA space suit. The suit was filled with oxygen so that she could breathe.

Calmly, Flo checked that the long tether on the suit was attached to the spacecraft. This rope would stop her from floating away. Alex lifted the SAFER onto her back.

"This is just in case the tether comes off," he reassured her.

Flo gave the thumbs-up to Izzy and Alex, and they left the capsule. Flo then pressed a button to open the air lock.

SAFER is like a backpack but has small jet thrusters. An astronaut controls the SAFER with a small joystick to get back to the spacecraft.

She stepped out into the darkness. It was like floating through water. She remembered her training for hours in the swimming pool back on Earth.

Ned spoke to her through the suit's radio. "How is *Ramesses* looking?"

"There are some dents," replied Flo. "I'll take a closer look." She floated over to inspect the marks. "They all seem fine," she reported back.

As she turned to return to the air lock, she caught a glimpse of a swirling globe. "Wow! Guys, have you spotted where we are?"

Inside *Ramesses*, the crew looked out to see an orb with bands of colour rippling around.

"It's the king of the planets, Jupiter!" said Lem excitedly.

Jupiter Data File

Location: fifth planet from the Sun

Landscape: thick layers of swirling gas clouds with a small core

Size: 11 times larger than Earth

Length of day: 9 Earth hours and 55 minutes

Length of year: 12 Earth years

Pulling power

The gravity of Jupiter is two and a half times stronger than Earth's gravity. This means that its pulling power affects space objects. More than 60 moons orbit Jupiter caught by its gravity.

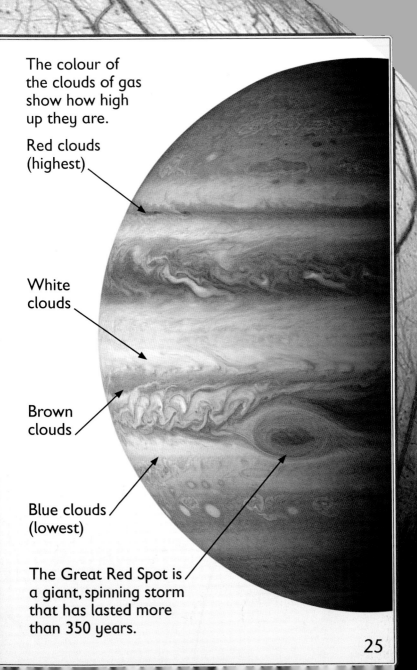

The colour of the clouds of gas show how high up they are.

Red clouds (highest)

White clouds

Brown clouds

Blue clouds (lowest)

The Great Red Spot is a giant, spinning storm that has lasted more than 350 years.

Jupiter Phase 1 Storm Surge

"Jupiter's huge!" gasped Alex as he gazed at the looming planet ahead. "Where do we start?"

"Those stormy clouds need checking out," suggested Izzy. "Let's release the robotic probe. It's too dangerous for us."

Lem took the controls of the probe. Izzy stood by the monitors to record the incoming data.

"It's away!" cried Lem as the probe detached from *Ramesses* and opened its antenna.

"The probe is detecting high levels of harmful rays," said Izzy.

"I'll activate the magnetic shield around *Ramesses*. This will protect us," said Ned.

The probe drifted closer and closer to Jupiter's cloud tops.

"Listen, guys!" said Izzy, excitedly. "The probe is picking up sound waves from the storms."

Strange noises came through the speakers. Coconut's ears perked up.

"That pecking sound is like woodpeckers tapping on tree trunks," remarked Alex.

"The hissing is like ocean waves crashing and it's as if whales are calling, too," added Flo.

"It's creepy music!" concluded Lem. "Look! Even Coconut finds it weird."

Everyone looked to see Coconut shaking her ears and scratching them with her hind legs.

Izzy swiftly turned the sound off and watched the monitors. "The probe is picking up a mix of gases in the clouds. It's mostly hydrogen with some helium—"

"Those are the two lightest gases in the universe," interrupted Alex.

"Yes, but the added dash of oxygen and nitrogen has made some interesting clouds," continued Izzy.

"Eeuch! That toxic air would choke us," said Lem, pulling a disgusted face.

"Wow, guys!" said Flo, pointing at a dancing, swirling blue glow. "There's some awesome light action over Jupiter's poles."

The gases above the north and south poles glow when the Sun's solar wind collides with them. These **auroras** are hundreds of times more powerful than those seen at Earth's poles.

"The probe's speeding up,"
alerted Lem. "I won't be able
to control it for much longer."

"It's been caught up in Jupiter's
high winds," said Izzy. She
watched as the speed dial rose
30,000 kph... 40,000 kph...
45,000 kph....

"It's being tossed around on
a mad swing ride," cried Alex.

"It's never going to survive
that hurricane!"

"It's being sucked down,
too," said Izzy. "The probe's
temperature is warming up."

Suddenly, the monitors' screens
fuzzed and then blacked out.

"Show's over, guys!" sighed
Lem. "The giant has either
crushed it or melted it or both."

Jupiter's Weather

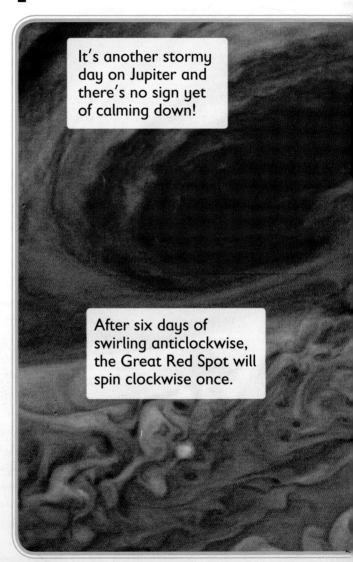

It's another stormy day on Jupiter and there's no sign yet of calming down!

After six days of swirling anticlockwise, the Great Red Spot will spin clockwise once.

The air around the equator will rise and flow to the poles after being warmed by the Sun.

The cooler air will flow back from the poles to the equator.

As usual, the speed of the clouds at the equator is more than 45,000 kph (28,000 mph) because Jupiter spins so fast.

Galileo Mission

5.3 m (17 ft) tall

Galileo was the name given to an unmanned spacecraft that was sent out to explore Jupiter and its moons. The spacecraft was named after Galileo Galilei, who used a telescope to observe Jupiter in 1610.

Galileo's timetable

18 October, 1989 Launched from the space shuttle *Atlantis*.

February, 1990 Flew past Venus and propelled into a new orbit.

July, 1995 Released probe. Five months later, the probe entered Jupiter's atmosphere. This was destroyed after 58 minutes in the heat and pressure.

December, 1995 Reached Jupiter to orbit the planet and its moons.

1997 Main mission completed.

21 September, 2003 Dropped into Jupiter and destroyed.

Jupiter Phase 2 Moon Missions

"Cheer up, guys!" said Ned. "We've loads more to explore. There are more than 60 moons going around Jupiter. How about we check out a few of them?"

"There's Ganymede, the largest one that's bigger than the planet Mercury," suggested Lem.

"Or sleepy, old, sparkling Callisto," added Flo.

"I'd like to try landing on the one that looks like a giant cheese pizza," said Alex.

"That's volcanic Io!" said Izzy. "Are you sure?"

"Yes," nodded Alex. "Let's find out what the lander *Juba* can do."

"It'll be dangerous," warned
Ned. "Those black spots are
active volcanoes. They could
erupt at any time."

"We'll land well away from
an active volcano," replied Alex.

"Who's up for taking *Juba* down there?"

"I'd like to pick up some sulphur rocks from Io's surface," said Izzy.

"I'll come to check that the space suits work ok," offered Flo. "The levels of harmful rays can change quickly. We don't want anyone to get ill."

Io looks yellow because the moon is covered with the mineral **sulphur**. This is yellow but turns red and then black when heated.

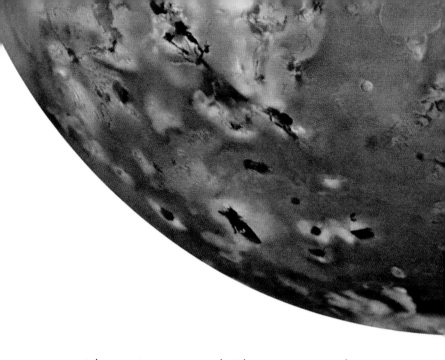

Alex, Izzy and Flo put on their
EVA suits before getting into
Juba. Alex took the controls.
He guided *Juba* away from
the dock and towards Io.

"There's nothing smooth to
land on," said Alex as they flew
closer. "We'll just topple over if

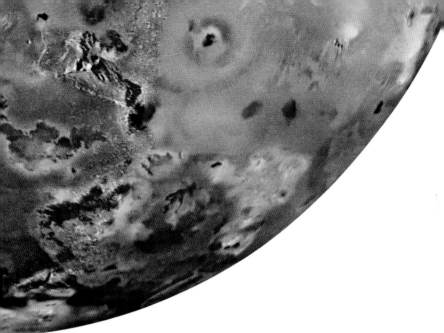

we try to land."

He flew *Juba* over the surface
of Io, searching. Some places
were covered in ash from
a recent volcanic eruption.
Other places were covered in
bumpy lumps of glistening
sulphur crystals.

"Look at that strange lava stack," pointed out Flo.

"Although the volcanoes are hot, the rest of the moon is cold," explained Izzy. "The lava cools very quickly, making these strange shapes."

44

"They make amazing sculptures," said Flo. "Let me take a photo."

"Be quick!" urged Alex. "We're a bit too close to that volcano. It looks a lively one!"

"Get out of here!" cried Izzy. "It's erupting. Back to *Ramesses*!"

As Alex sped *Juba* away, ash spurted from the volcano. It formed an enormous dome as it fell.

Volcanic eruptions on Io are different from those on Earth. The ash forms a dome as it falls because of the moon's low gravity.

Moon Zoom

These are Jupiter's four largest moons:

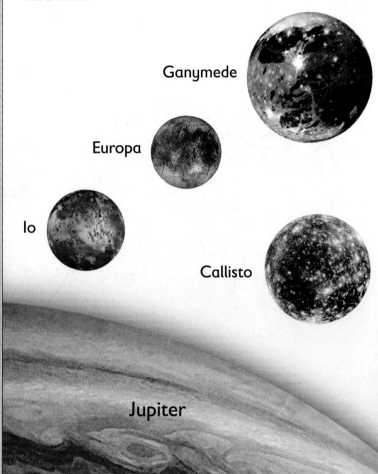

Ganymede

Europa

Io

Callisto

Jupiter

Ganymede

Rock and ice cover this large moon. Dark areas are very old craters and lighter areas show unusual grooves.

Callisto

This icy moon is said to be the most cratered object in the solar system. The glowing light areas are craters.

Io

This sulphur-covered moon is the most volcanically active object in our solar system.

Europa

This young moon has a flat icy surface that appears like broken ice floating on an ocean.

47

Jupiter Phase 3
Icy World

"Phew! We made it back,"
said Alex, as he docked *Juba*.
    "Where to now?" asked Lem,
as he met them at the hatch.
"I don't want to miss out on
the next adventure."

"My heart's still pounding," said Flo. "I'm not going anywhere."

"I still need some samples," said Izzy. "Shall we try the icy moon Europa? Scientists think there could be life in a salty ocean under the ice."

"Hop in, Lem," said Alex. "Let's go!" He restarted *Juba's* engines and moved the lander away from the dock.

"This landing is going to be slippery," warned Alex.

"It'll be like landing on moving ice in the Arctic," added Izzy. "The ice is always shifting because of the ocean underneath. Those cracks open up and then close again."

"Let's hope we don't fall into one," said Lem, crossing his fingers.

Alex pressed a button to inflate the air bags under *Juba*. As the lander hit the ice, the air bags softened the impact. But *Juba* began to slide and skid across the ice.

"*Juba* isn't slowing down and we're heading for that crack!" Alex gasped.

Just in time, *Juba* stopped on the edge of the crack. The crew sighed with relief.

"It's too cold for us to go outside," said Izzy. "We'll control the cryobot from inside. We need to drop it down through the ice, fill it up with a water sample, and then bring it back up before the crack shifts. We'll have to time this exactly."

"Leave it to me," said Lem confidently. Slowly he lowered the cryobot on a winch down through the ice. "10 km... 20 km... 30 km...."

Splash!

"35 km! It's reached the ocean," Izzy said excitedly.

A **cryobot** is a device that can drill through ice. Inside it has hot water, which heats the rounded head. This then melts the ice as it travels down and back up.

The crew watched the screen
as the cryobot swam around.
The ocean was a clear icy blue.

"Nothing," said Izzy,
disappointed.

"Wait for it!" said Lem.

Suddenly a patch of dark blue
whisked across the screen.

"What was that?" asked Alex.

Lem turned the camera on the cryobot, searching for the splodge. But the splodge found them. A strange-looking mouth and eyes peered into the camera lens.

"Cool!" exclaimed Lem.

"The ice is breaking up!" cried Izzy. "We haven't much time left. Let's collect the water sample and get the cryobot out of there."

Lem hoisted the cryobot back up through the ice. Alex fired up *Juba's* engines ready to make a speedy launch.

CRACK!

Juba juddered as the ice underneath the lander shifted.

"We need to go!" shouted Alex.

"One second more... Yes! The cryobot is back on board," announced Lem.

Juba lifted off and headed back to *Ramesses*.

As Lem peered into the water sample, the blue blob stared back at him.

"Splodge came too!" laughed Lem. "It can be my Space Quest pet. Our next stop is Saturn."

Gas Facts

Gas is a substance that has no shape. These four gases have no smell and no taste at room temperature. They are in the air around us but can't be seen.

Hydrogen is the lightest gas and the most common one in the universe. It is in water.

Helium is the second lightest gas and the second most common one in the universe.

Oxygen is the third most common gas in the universe. It is needed by most life forms on Earth to survive.

Nitrogen makes up around 78 per cent of the air we breathe. It is found in all life forms on Earth.

Jupiter Quiz

1. Why are asteroids covered in craters?

2. What is the Great Red Spot on Jupiter?

3. How many Earth years make a year on Jupiter?

4. Why does the moon Io look like a cheese pizza?

5. What did Lem use to get through the ice on Europa?

Answers on page 61.

Glossary

activate
to turn on

atmosphere
layer of gases
surrounding
a planet

aurora
natural light effect
in the sky

crater
hollow made by
an explosion or
a crash

equator
invisible line
around the centre
of a planet

gravity
force that pulls
objects towards
each other

inflate
to fill up with air
or gas

laser
narrow beam of
powerful light

magnetic shield
invisible screen
that protects from
harmful rays

orbit
curved path around
a planet or a star

probe
device that
investigates
unknown areas

sample
small collection
of something
for studying

Index

Answers to the Jupiter Quiz:

1. They've crashed into each other; **2.** A giant storm that has lasted more than 350 years; **3.** 12 Earth years; **4.** Io is covered in sulphur; **5.** A cryobot.

Guide for Parents

DK Reads is a three-level interactive reading adventure series for children, developing the habit of reading widely for both pleasure and information. These chapter books have an exciting main narrative interspersed with a range of reading genres to suit your child's reading ability, as required by the National Curriculum. Each book is designed to develop your child's reading skills, fluency, grammar awareness, and comprehension in order to build confidence and engagement when reading.

Ready for a *Starting to Read Alone* book

YOUR CHILD SHOULD

- be able to read most words without needing to stop and break them down into sound parts.
- read smoothly, in phrases and with expression. By this level, your child will be mostly reading silently.
- self-correct when some word or sentence doesn't sound right.

A VALUABLE AND SHARED READING EXPERIENCE

For some children, text reading, particularly non-fiction, requires much effort but adult participation can make this both fun and easier. So here are a few tips on how to use this book with your child.

TIP 1 Check out the contents together before your child begins:

- invite your child to check the blurb, contents page and layout of the book and comment on it.
- ask your child to make predictions about the story.
- chat about the information your child might want to find out.

TIP 2 Encourage fluent and flexible reading:

- support your child to read in fluent, expressive phrases, making full use of punctuation and thinking about the meaning.

- encourage your child to slow down and check information where appropriate.

TIP 3 Indicators that your child is reading for meaning:

- your child will be responding to the text if he/she is self-correcting and varying his/her voice.

- your child will want to chat about what he/she is reading or is eager to turn the page to find out what will happen next.

TIP 4 Praise, share and chat:

- the factual pages tend to be more difficult than the story pages, and are designed to be shared with your child.

- encourage your child to recall specific details after each chapter.

- provide opportunities for your child to pick out interesting words and discuss what they mean.

- discuss how the author captures the reader's interest, or how effective the non-fiction layouts are.

- ask questions about the text. These help to develop comprehension skills and awareness of the language used.

A FEW ADDITIONAL TIPS

- Read to your child regularly to demonstrate fluency, phrasing and expression; to find out or check information; and for sharing enjoyment.

- Encourage your child to reread favourite texts to increase reading confidence and fluency.

- Check that your child is reading a range of different types, such as poems, jokes and following instructions.

Series consultant **Shirley Bickler** is a longtime advocate of carefully crafted, enthralling texts for young readers. Her LIFT initiative for infant teaching was the model for the National Literacy Strategy Literacy Hour, and she is co-author of *Book Bands for Guided Reading* published by Reading Recovery based at the Institute of Education.

Have you read these other great books from DK?

STARTING TO READ ALONE

Discover what it takes to become a professional football player.

Design and test a rocket for a spying mission. Try out some experiments.

Embark on a mission to explore the solar system. First stop – Mars.

READING ALONE

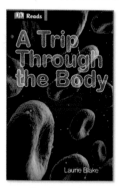

Explore the amazing systems at work inside the human body.

Step back nearly 20,000 years to the days of early cave dwellers.

Encounter the rare animals in the mountain forests of Cambodia.